# TRICKY ALEX

*Written by Morgan Matthews*
*Illustrated by Ben Mahan*

**Troll Associates**

*Library of Congress Cataloging in Publication Data*

Matthews, Morgan.
Tricky Alex.

Summary: His friends try to convince Alex the elf that they do not like him to play tricks on them.
[1. Fairies—Fiction. 2. Behavior—Fiction]
I. Mahan, Ben, ill. II. Title.
PZ7.M43425Tr 1986 [E] 85-14018
ISBN 0-8167-0598-4 (lib. bdg.)
ISBN 0-8167-0599-2 (pbk.)


Printed in the United States of America

10 9 8 7 6 5 4 3 2 1

# TRICKY ALEX

Alex was an elf. He was a tricky elf. He liked to play tricks on everybody.

Alex had a lot of friends. He played tricks on his friends. And some of his tricks were not very nice.

Alex played a trick on Mr. Wizard. The little elf hid by the brook. Along came Mr. Wizard. He did not see Alex.

Out jumped the elf.
"BOO!" yelled Alex.
SPLASH! Into the brook went Mr. Wizard. Into the mud he fell. What a naughty trick!

Tricks! Tricks! Tricks! Alex played a lot of tricks. He tricked Gus Goblin. He tricked Emily Elf. Alex even played a trick on Goodie Goodwitch.

Goodie Goodwitch had some ducks. She liked to use duck eggs in her witch's brew.
Alex hid by the ducks.
"This will be a good trick," he said.
Along came Goodie. Her arms were full of eggs.

"BOO! BOO! BOO!" yelled Alex.
Goodie Goodwitch jumped. Up went the eggs. Down they went. SPLAT! SPLAT! SPLAT! Eggs splattered everywhere.

"Oh no!" said Goodie. "What a mess! What a bad trick to play!"
Alex looked at the mess.
"I am tricky," said Alex. "But I am not a bad elf. I will clean up the eggs."

Goodie looked at Alex.
"It was a bad trick," she said.
"But I still like you. My magic will clean up the mess. My magic wand will do the cleaning."

Out came Goodie's magic wand.
"Now you will see a good trick,"
Goodie said.
The witch tapped the splattered
eggs.
"Mess, vanish!" she said.

BOOM! What good magic! The mess vanished. The splattered eggs were gone.

"What a trick!" Alex yelled. "I cannot see the eggs. Are the eggs invisible?"

Goodie Goodwitch looked at the elf.

"The mess is not invisible. It is gone. But I *can* make things invisible. Look at this duck."

Alex watched. Goodie tapped the duck with her wand. BOOM! The duck disappeared.

"The duck is invisible," said the witch. "It is here. But you cannot see it."

*Quack, quack!* Alex heard the duck. He looked and looked. But he could not see anything.

"I like this trick," he said.

"Watch again," said Goodie. She tapped the invisible duck with the wand. BOOM! The duck was now visible. It could be seen.

“I would like to be invisible,” said Alex. “An invisible elf could play a lot of tricks. Will you make me invisible?”

Goodie thought about making Alex invisible. Would it be a good thing to do? She thought and thought. Goodie thought up a plan.

"I will make you invisible," she laughed.
Goodie tapped Alex with the wand. But she did not do real magic.

“Am I invisible?” asked Alex.
Goodie laughed.
“I cannot see you,” the witch said.
But she could see him. Alex Elf was visible.

Goodie had a good plan. She was going to trick Alex. All of Alex's friends would trick him, too.
"Only you can see yourself," said Goodie. "To everyone else you are invisible."
Alex laughed.
"Good," he said.
Away went Invisible Alex.

Goodie went to see Mr. Wizard. She went to see Gus Goblin and Emily Elf. Everyone liked Goodie's plan. Everyone laughed and laughed.

"So Alex is now invisible,"
laughed Mr. Wizard.
"What a good plan," said Emily.
"What a funny trick," said Gus.
They all went away laughing.

Alex was going by the brook. He saw Mr. Wizard.
"I will trick him," said Invisible Alex. "I do not even have to hide. I cannot be seen. I will surprise him."

Alex thought he was invisible. But he was visible! Mr. Wizard saw him. But he pretended not to see the elf. Alex jumped up. "BOO," he yelled. Mr. Wizard ducked.

SPLASH! Into the brook went Alex. Mr. Wizard laughed. Away he went.
"That trick was not very nice," said Alex. "I tricked myself."

Out of the brook came Alex. So far, being invisible was not much fun. And Alex wanted to have fun. He wanted to trick someone.

Alex went to see Gus Goblin. Gus was playing in the mud. He liked mud. Gus was making mud pies.

“This will be fun,” said Alex. “An invisible elf can play a lot of funny tricks. I will make Gus jump.”

Up to Gus went Alex. Gus saw the elf coming. But he pretended he did not see Alex. Gus had a plan.

"BOO! BOO!" yelled Alex.
Gus jumped. Up went a mud pie. Down it went. Where did it go?

SPLAT! SPLAT! SPLAT!
The mud splattered all over Alex.
Mud here! Mud there! What a
mess! Away went a muddy,
invisible elf.

"This is not good," said Alex. "My tricks are not very funny. I will go see Emily Elf. I like Emily."

Emily Elf was with Goodie Goodwitch. Emily and Goodie were having pie. Emily was a very good pie-maker.

"Pie!" said Alex. "I like Emily's pies. I do not want to be tricky now."
Alex went up to Emily.

“May I have some pie?” asked Alex.
Emily laughed. She looked around.
“Who said that?” asked Emily.
“Who asked for pie?”

“I did not ask for pie,” said Goodie.
“I did!” yelled Alex.
“Who are you?” asked Emily.

"I am Alex Elf," Alex said.
"Where are you?" asked Emily.
"I cannot see you. Is this a trick?"

"Oh no," yelled Alex. "Goodie used her magic wand on me. The magic made me invisible. No one can see me."

"I can see you," said Mr. Wizard.
He had come for pie.
"I can see you, too," said Gus Goblin.
He had come for pie.

"Do you mean I am *not* invisible?" asked Alex.
"That's right," said Goodie. "I played a trick on you. I did not use real magic."
Emily laughed.
"We all played a trick on you," she said.

Alex laughed.
"I thought it was funny to be tricky," he said. "But I do not like tricks anymore. I will never play another trick on my friends."

"Good for you!" said Alex's friends.
"Now let's all have pie," said Emily.

Everyone got some pie. The pie looked good. Alex looked at his pie. He laughed.

"Watch this," said A[illegible] "Now *I* will do magic! I wi[illegible] pie vanish."
And he did!